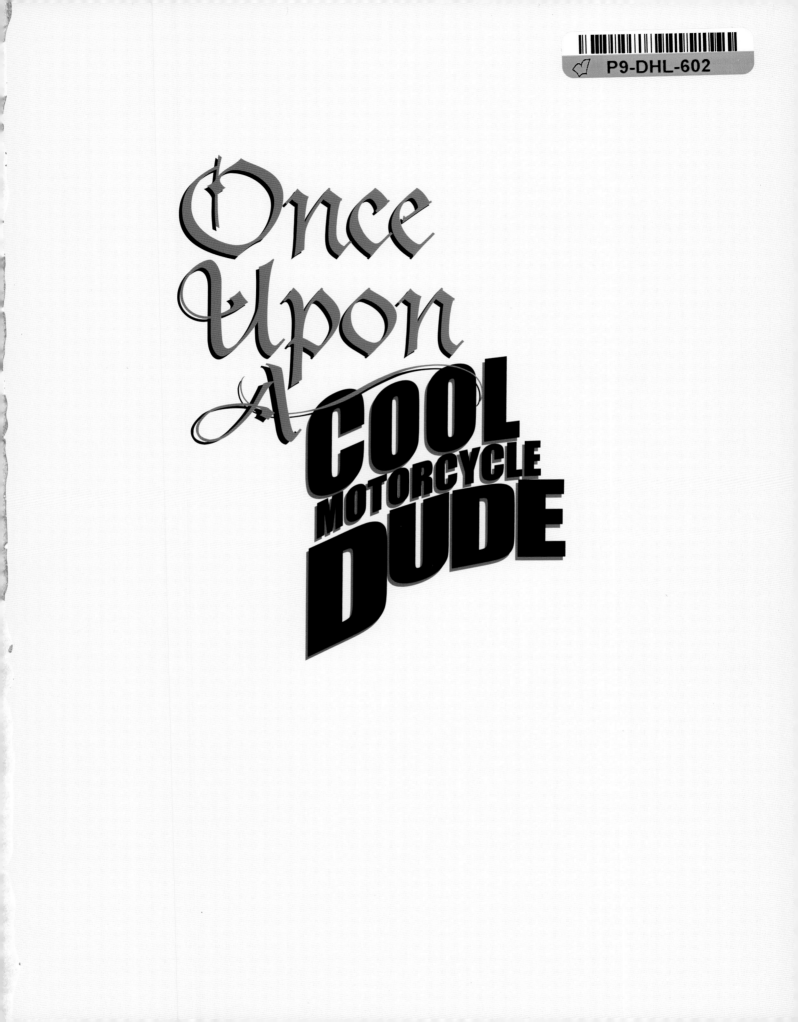

For Scott Goto, Carol Heyer, and Cathy Evans.
—K. O.

For my godchildren, Chase Atkinson, Skylar Rae Atkinson,
Julia Ruiz, and Jessica Boudville. And, as always, to my
parents, William J. and Merlyn M. Heyer.
—C. H.

For all my bike-riding and non-bike-riding Dudes and
Dudettes, whom I call my friends.
—S. G.

Text copyright © 2005 by Kevin O'Malley
Illustrations copyright © 2005 by Kevin O'Malley, Carol Heyer, and Scott Goto

First published in the United States of America in 2005
by Walker Books for Young Readers, an imprint of Bloomsbury Publishing, Inc.
www.bloomsbury.com

For information about permission to reproduce selections from this book, write to
Permissions, Walker BFYR, 1385 Broadway, New York, New York 10018
Bloomsbury books may be purchased for business or promotional use. For information on bulk
purchases please contact Macmillan Corporate and Premium Sales Department at
specialmarkets@macmillan.com

Library of Congress Cataloging-in-Publication Data
O'Malley, Kevin.
Once upon a cool motorcycle dude / written and illustrated by Kevin O'Malley ;
illustrated by Carol Heyer ; illustrated by Scott Gogo.
p.   cm.
Summary: Cooperatively writing a fairy tale for school, a girl imagines a beautiful
princess whose beloved ponies are being stolen by a giant, and a boy conjures
up the muscular biker who will guard the last pony in exchange for gold.
ISBN-13: 978-0-8027-8947-1 • ISBN-10: 0-8027-8947-1 (hardcover)
ISBN-13: 978-0-8027-8949-5 • ISBN-10: 0-8027-8949-8 (reinforced)
[1. Authorship—Fiction. 2. Princesses—Fiction. 3. Motorcyclists—Fiction. 4. Giants—Fiction.
5. Fairy tales. 6. Humorous stories.] I. Heyer, Carol, ill. II. Goto, Scott, ill. III. Title.
PZ8.O565 On 2005   [Fic]—dc22   2004053613

Kevin O'Malley used pen and ink and digital color, Scott Goto used acrylic and oil on paper,
and Carol Heyer used acrylics to create the illustrations for this book.
Book design by Cathy Evans/Shoot the Moon

Printed in China by C&C Offset Printing Co., Ltd., Shenzhen, Guangdong
16 18 20 19 17 15 (hardcover)
6 8 10 9 7 5 (reinforced)

All papers used by Bloomsbury Publishing, Inc., are natural, recyclable products
made from wood grown in well-managed forests. The manufacturing processes
conform to the environmental regulations of the country of origin.

Once upon a time in a castle on a hill there lived a beautiful princess named Princess Tenderheart.

Every day Princess Tenderheart would play
with her eight beautiful ponies. She named
them Jasmie, Nimble, Sophie, and Polly.
And Penny and Sunny and Monica . . .

Her favorite pony of all
was called Buttercup.

One night a terrible thing happened. A giant came and stole away poor little Jasmie. All the other ponies cried and cried, but Princess Tenderheart cried hardest of all.

It was very sad.

The very next night the giant came and took Nimble and Sophie. Princess Tenderheart cried all day and refused to eat.

Oh please . . . get a grip, Princess!

Her father, the king, hired all the princes he could find to protect the ponies, but night after night another pony was stolen away.

The poor princess just sat in her room and turned straw into gold thread. She cried and cried and cried. When only Buttercup was left, Princess Tenderheart thought her heart would break.

Oh, who would protect Buttercup?

That's it . . . I can't take it anymore. I'll tell the story from here.

One day this really cool muscle dude rides up to the castle on his motorcycle. He says he'll guard the last pony if the king gives him all the gold thread that the princess makes. The king says okay, and the dude sits and waits for the giant.

As if . . .
He's not even cute or anything.

So that night the giant heads up to the castle. Man, this giant was an ugly dude. He was big and mean and he had four teeth in his mouth that were all rotten and yellow and black . . .

. . . and his breath smelled like rotten, moldy, stinky wet feet.

That's just gross!

He needs eight ponies to make a tasty pony stew and he only has seven. So that night he goes to steal the last horsey.

The muscle dude has this really big sword.
The giant and the dude battled all over the
place. The Earth was shaking and there
was lightning and thunder and volcanoes
were exploding.

It was HUGE!

Volcanoes? Where'd the volcanoes come from?

Night after night the giant comes back, but the dude beats him. Night after night the princess makes gold thread and gives it to the dude. He gets really RICH . . .

Princess Tenderheart goes to the gym and pumps iron.
She becomes **Princess Warrior**.

VERY COOL!

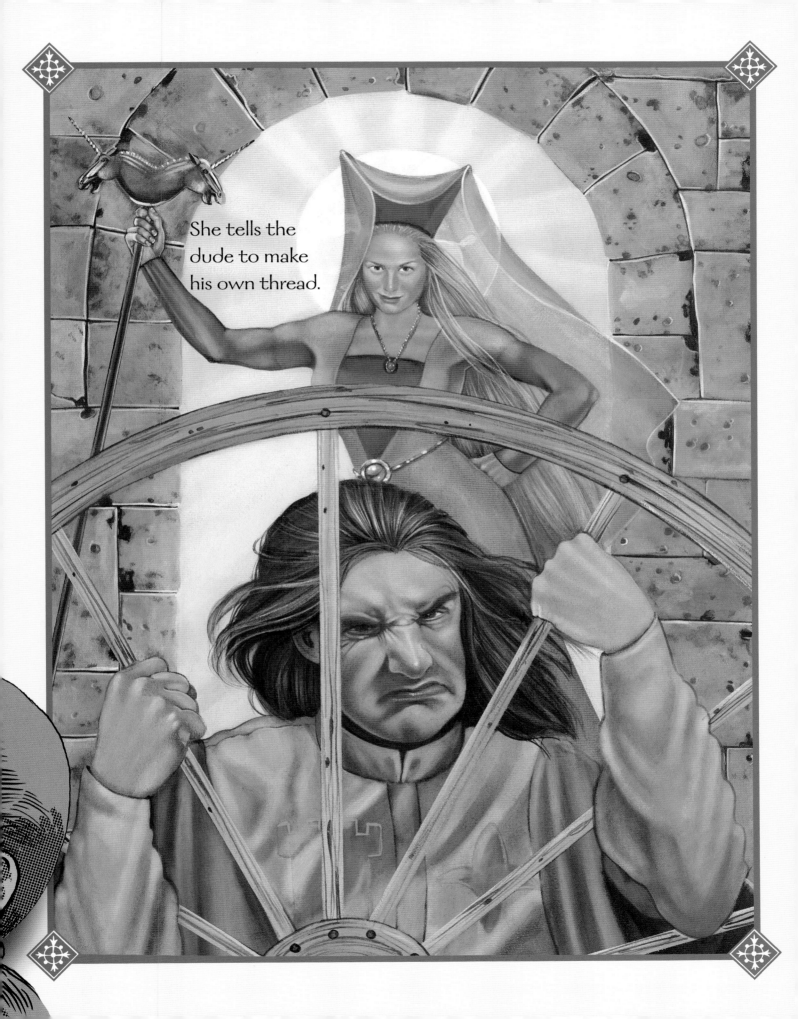

So that night the princess has this huge and tremendous battle. The giant runs back to his cave.

The End.

The dude makes this really cool blanket
out of the gold thread, and when he
puts it over his head he turns INVISIBLE.
Then he goes to rescue the ponies.

You can't see me!

The dude and the princess get into this big fight over who gets to free the ponies. *The giant hears voices and gets so scared he jumps off the cliff.*

The End.

	DATE DUE